Dr. Gardner's
STORIES
ABOUT THE
REAL
WORLD

Volume II

Dr. Gardner's
STORIES
ABOUT THE
REAL
WORLD

Volume II

RICHARD A. GARDNER, M.D.
Clinical Professor of Child Psychiatry
Columbia University, College of Physicians and Surgeons

Illustrations by
ROBERT MYERS

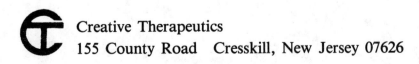
Creative Therapeutics
155 County Road   Cresskill, New Jersey 07626

Library of Congress Cataloging in Publication Data (Revised)

Gardner, Richard A
  Dr. Gardner's stories about the real world.

  Vol. 2: Illustrations by Robert Myers.
  Vol. 1: Reprint of the 1972 ed. published by Prentice-
Hall, Englewood Cliffs, N.J.
  SUMMARY: Twelve stories which present realistic
solutions to common childhood problems and
situations, such as avoiding responsibility,
wishing for a pet, or dealing with bullies.
  1. Children's stories, American. [1. Behavior—
Fiction. 2. Conduct of life—Fiction. 3. Short
stories] I. Lowenheim, Alfred.
II. Myers, Robert. III. Title.
IV. Title: Stories about the real world.
[PZ7.G17932Do 1980]   [Fic]   80–16542
ISBN 0-933812-04-3 (v. 1)
ISBN 0-933812-05-1 (v. 2)

Copyright ©1983 by Creative Therapeutics.

Illustrations copyright by Robert Myers.

PRINTED IN THE UNITED STATES OF AMERICA

To my son
Andrew Kevin

*For giving me gratifications
beyond my dreams*

CONTENTS

ACKNOWLEDGMENTS

I am deeply indebted to the children whose enthusiastic responses to the first volume of these stories served as an impetus to my writing this second series.

Once again, Dr. Frances Dubner lent invaluable assistance through her astute evaluation of the original manuscript and her penetrating suggestions. Mr. Robert Myers, who provided sensitive illustrations to my book of fables, has once again demonstrated his talent with poignant illustrations that have enhanced the text immeasurably. Mrs. Linda Gould, my secretary, has once again proved her devotion to the typing and editing of my work. I am extremely grateful to Mrs. Barbara Christenberry for her dedication from the editing of the original manuscript to carrying the book through its various phases of production. The final product is a statement of her skill.

OTHER BOOKS BY RICHARD A. GARDNER

INTRODUCTION
FOR
ADULTS

If I simply count the number of books sold, I cannot consider my original *Stories About the Real World* a runaway success; but it certainly was not a failure either. It did go through two Prentice-Hall printings and is presently doing reasonably well as a Creative Therapeutics' publication. The paperback sales (published by Avon Books and now Creative Therapeutics) have been slow but steady. These printings, however, give no information about the number of books sold, a figure which is presently about 10,000. More important than printings and number, however, has been the response of individual children to the book. It has been second only to the response to my *The Boys and Girls Book About Divorce* in enthusiasm children have shown. For many it has been like a good friend. For others it has been a reference book to help them deal with difficult situations. Some have placed it under their pillows at night, like a security blanket. Naturally, such responses are an immense source of pleasure to me as an author. And such reactions prompted my writing this second book of stories in this genre.

The storytelling medium is one of the most potent, if not the most potent, ways to impart important messages to children. It appears to be the child's natural mode of communication. Simply stated facts are far less attractive to children than facts embellished by the fanciful tale. The excitement of stories provides what Mary Poppins described as the "spoonful of sugar" that helps the medicine go down. And unpleasant facts are much more likely to be "heard" when presented in a format in which *others,* rather than the children themselves, are the perpetrators of the unacceptable behavior.

An important, if not the main, determinant of whether children will like a particular story is the capacity to identify with the protagonist. If the issues dealt with are those that the children themselves are being confronted with at the time, then they are likely to become involved via identification with the primary character(s). If not, they will soon become distracted and will find the story boring. In this book, as was true for its predecessor, I have tried to select themes of universal interest to enhance the likelihood that children will become involved. Each story deals with common, if not universal, issues with which all children must deal. Throughout, the approach to solving each problem is practical and realistic, but in no way simplistic. These stories, unlike fairy tales, do not provide magical solutions. They do, however, provide real solutions that can work—if the child is willing to utilize them. These messages, then, if incorporated into the child's psychic structure, are likely to induce adequate functioning in the real, rather than the unreal, world. And such realistic adaptation is one of the most important aims of the child-rearing process. My hope is that this second volume will be as successful as the first in contributing (admittedly in a small way) toward the attainment of this goal.

THE ESKIMO BOYS AND THE FISH

Way up north, in the Arctic, there lived two Eskimo boys named Eski and Kimo. They were very good friends and lived near one another. Life in the land where they lived was very difficult. It was not only very cold, especially in the winter time, but it was very hard to get food. In the winter, especially, food was very scarce.

One of the most important foods that the Eskimos eat is fish. Of course, the Eskimos have to go out and catch their fish. Fish just don't jump out of the water and say to the Eskimos, "Please eat me." Nor do any of the fish say, "Please catch me with your spear." Nor do any of them say, "Please fool me with bait on the line of your fishing pole, so that I'll bite it and you'll pull me out of the water." Nor do any of them say, "Please tell me where your fish nets are so I can swim into them and get caught."

Actually, the fish are very hard to catch and they try to avoid being caught by the Eskimos. In the winter they are especially difficult to catch because of the ice that covers the water. Then the Eskimos have to make holes in the ice and catch the fish through them. And so catching fish in the winter is even harder than catching them in the summer.

Both Eski's and Kimo's fathers worked very hard to give their families enough food to eat. However, their fathers were different on the subject of whether their sons should work so hard as well. Eski's father often said, "It's very important for children to learn how to catch fish when they're very young. They have to start to learn the importance of hard work when they're young or else they may never learn. Of course, childhood is also a time for some fun as well. Both work and play are important."

Kimo's father, on the other hand, used to say, "I want my children to have an easier life than I've had. Childhood is a time for fun—and only fun. They'll learn to fish when they get older."

And so both boys spent time having fun. But when they weren't together, Eski's father took him hunting and fishing with him and taught Eski many things about how to hunt and fish. Although it was often hard

work, it made Eski feel very good about himself when he caught a fish or animal.

However, when Eski was learning how to do all these things, Kimo found other boys and girls to play with. For him, childhood was supposed to be only fun and he didn't want to miss out on one minute of it. Kimo never had to worry about having food because he knew that his father was always going to give him enough to eat. When Eski told Kimo that catching fish could be a lot of fun, Kimo didn't believe it. And when Eski told Kimo that the hard work was worth it because you felt so good about yourself for having done something difficult, Kimo laughed and thought Eski must be "sick in the head."

And so the years went on. Year after year Kimo played and enjoyed himself. And year after year Eski

spent some time playing and some time working and learning.

Finally, they became teen-agers. One day Kimo's father told his son that it was time for him to learn how to fish and hunt and do all the other things that Eskimo men do to get food for their families. He told Kimo that he would like him to come along on the next fishing trip in order to learn how to fish. Kimo said, "But I'm only a teen-ager. I'm too young to do all that work."

"But you're almost a man now," said his father. "You're as big and strong as a man, and it's time you started to learn how to work like a man."

"I don't wanna do it," cried Kimo. "Work's no fun. And besides," Kimo said to his father, "you're a good fisherman and hunter and you're still young. So why won't you just continue to get food for me and the rest of the family?"

No matter how hard Kimo's father tried to convince him of the importance of learning how to do these things, it did no good. And the more he tried to get Kimo to go with him, in order to learn how to do these things, the more Kimo refused to move. Besides, Kimo was so big now that his father couldn't force him to go. And so he just left him there.

As time passed, Kimo still refused to learn how to fish and hunt. He began to find himself very lonely because all of his friends were now grown, and they were all hunting and fishing and taking care of the families that they now started to have. Even Kimo's old friend Eski had little to do with him. Eski found that he had less and less to talk about with Kimo because Eski was out all day doing things and sometimes even having adventures. Kimo, on the other hand, was leading a very boring and uninteresting life.

In the end, Kimo never learned how to hunt and fish. People felt sorry for him and gave him some food because they didn't want him to starve. But he never got the best parts of the fish and animals that were hunted. And he never felt the good feeling that comes from having done something well.

Lessons:
1) When you work for something, you feel good about yourself for the accomplishment. When something is given to you, you don't feel so good about yourself.
2) The caught fish is tastier than the one that someone else catches.
3) Give a man a fish, and you've given him a meal. Teach a man how to fish, and you've given him a meal for life.
4) Both work and play are important if you are to be satisfied with your life.

THE BOY, THE MONKEY, AND THE BANANA MACHINE

Once there was a scientist. A scientist does experiments to learn about the world and to improve it. Often a scientist works in a place called a laboratory. In her laboratory, this scientist once built a special kind of machine. In the front was a small hole called a slot. There was also a big hole in the front as well. In the back the scientist put many bananas. Every time a coin was put in the slot, a banana would come out of the big hole in the front of the machine. The only way someone could get a banana from the machine was to put in a coin.

One day, the scientist brought a monkey to the laboratory. This monkey, like most monkeys, loved bananas. She taught the monkey how to use her machine. Very soon he learned that every time he put a coin in the slot, a banana would come out of the machine.

On another day the scientist brought a little boy to the laboratory. This boy liked bananas very much. The scientist taught him how to put coins in the machine in order to get bananas. Each time he got a banana he was very happy.

Before long, both the monkey and the little boy learned well how to work the machine. Each would keep putting coins in the machine as long as he wanted a banana. And each liked bananas very much.

Then one day the scientist decided to do another experiment. She took all the bananas out of the machine. So then, when anyone put a coin in the machine, nothing came out.

When the monkey came to the laboratory, he immediately went over to the machine and put in a coin. Nothing happened. And so he put in another coin. Again, nothing happened. The monkey looked very disappointed. He put in a few more coins and still no bananas came out. And so the monkey stopped trying to get bananas out of the machine. Even though there was still a big pile of coins next to the machine, he didn't even put in one more. He seemed to have learned that putting coins in the machine was not going to get him any more bananas.

Then the little boy came to the laboratory. He too went right over to the machine and put in a coin. Nothing came out. So he put in another coin. Again, nothing came out. He started to get very angry. He put in another coin. And again nothing came out. Then he started to kick the machine, hoping that this would make it give bananas. But still nothing came out. He screamed at the machine, banged it with his fists, and

started having a temper tantrum. Again, no bananas came out of the machine. Finally, he screamed at the machine and started calling it dirty names. But still no bananas came out.

But the boy did not give up hope. He continued putting more coins into the machine. But still no bananas. And he kept on screaming and crying and putting in coins. No matter how loudly he screamed and no matter how hard he kicked the machine, no bananas came out. Finally they had to drag him out of the laboratory, angry, screaming, and kicking because he didn't get any bananas.

Lessons:
1) If at first you don't succeed, try, try again. If after that, you still don't succeed, forget it! Don't make a big fool of yourself.
2) Human beings like to think that they are smarter than monkeys. Are you?

JEFFREY, JULIE, AND THE CIGARETTES

Jeffrey was very happy. It was his 13th birthday. Now he was a teen-ager. When he was younger he always thought how great it would be to be a teen-ager. And now the day had finally come.

A few weeks before his birthday, his parents decided to have a party for him. They asked him whom he wished to invite. "I don't want anyone who isn't a teen-ager," said Jeffrey. "I don't want any little 11 or 12 year olds at my party. I'm a teen-ager now and I'm only going to have big kids at my party."

And so when the day of the party arrived, only teen-agers came. Before long, some of them started to smoke cigarettes. Now Jeffrey had never smoked before. In fact, he didn't even like the smell of cigarette smoke. Sometimes it even made him choke and sick to his stomach. But the kids who were smoking looked

really *big* to Jeffrey. He thought that everyone was admiring the boys and girls who were smoking. And so, when one of them offered Jeffrey a cigarette, he took it.

When he took his first puff, Jeffrey thought the taste was very, very bitter. In fact, he thought it was disgusting. Also, it was very hard for him to breathe. There was so much smoke in his nose, mouth, and throat that he thought he was going to choke. However, he didn't

want the others to think that he was a baby. He didn't want them to think that smoking bothered him and so he covered up his feelings. He tried to make believe that it didn't bother him. In fact, he went further and tried to make believe that he actually enjoyed it—when he really hated it.

After a few puffs, Jeffrey began to feel sick. But he didn't want anyone to know how he felt. He was sure that the others would think that he was a baby if they knew that he got sick from smoking.

Jeffrey then said that he had to go to the bathroom. As he got closer to the bathroom he felt so sick in his stomach that he thought that he was going to vomit. And so, he ran as fast as he could, hoping that no one knew what was happening. As soon as he got into the

bathroom he began to vomit in the toilet. In fact, he almost didn't make it to the bathroom and he was lucky that he didn't vomit on the floor.

After a while, Jeffrey felt better. During the rest of the party he kept admiring the boys and girls who could smoke. He wished that he could smoke without getting sick, and he promised himself that he would someday smoke like the others.

The next day, when school was let out, Jeffrey stopped off at a store and bought a pack of cigarettes. He lied and told the store owner that they were for his mother, because he knew that the storekeeper would not sell them to him because of his age. Jeffrey then ran home with his first pack of cigarettes.

He knew that no one would be home because he was an only child and his mother and father worked. They usually didn't come home until supper time. As soon as he got to his house, he went to the bathroom and decided to practice his smoking. First, he stood in front of the mirror in order to watch himself use the cigarette. He didn't light it yet. He wanted to practice the motions of smoking a cigarette. He wanted to hold the cigarette the way grownups do, the way someone would after smoking for a long time. He thought about how grownups look when they smoked and hoped that he would look just the way they do.

He kept putting the cigarette in his mouth in many different ways in order to get it *just right*. And he kept taking it out of his mouth and putting it back in, just the way grownups do. He stood there a long time, just

practicing with the unlit cigarette. He stayed there so long that he didn't realize how late it was getting. He suddenly heard his mother coming into the house. He quickly put the cigarette into his pocket and walked out of the bathroom. As he said hello to his mother he tried to make believe that nothing had happened.

The next day Jeffrey once again came right home from school and locked himself in the bathroom. Again, he practiced using the unlit cigarette. After a few days of such practice, he felt that he had finally learned well the motions of smoking. He thought that no one would be able to tell that he had just learned how to do it.

Next came the hardest part—actually smoking the cigarette. He knew that it was going to make him sick at first, but he knew also that he would get used to cigarettes. He knew that each time he smoked, cigarettes would bother him less and less. And so he lit the cigarette and started to puff. Immediately he began to cough and gasp. Soon he felt like vomiting. But he was not going to stop. He knew that he would get used to cigarettes, if he just kept smoking. As he smoked, he thought about how much of a big shot everyone would think he was when he could smoke like a grownup. When he would think of this, he would forget—for a minute—how sick the cigarettes were making him. He also thought about how impressed all the girls would be with him if he smoked and how they would look up to him as a big shot. And this made it easier for him to continue to suffer from the smoke.

Every afternoon Jeffrey went home and every afternoon he practiced his smoking. It took him a long time, and he got sick to his stomach many times but, as he had expected, he finally got used to smoking cigarettes. In fact, he could not count the number of times he coughed and choked before he finally got used to cigarette smoke.

Finally the day came when Jeffrey was so used to smoking that he didn't get sick at all and he didn't find

the taste of cigarettes disgusting. In addition, he practiced smoking until he was sure that he looked like an
"expert." Then he thought that he was finally ready to
smoke in front of others. So he decided to try smoking
first in the boy's bathroom at school. He knew that a
lot of kids sneaked into that room to smoke and that he
could learn more about smoking from other kids his
age.

And this is what happened. He went to the boy's room and practiced his smoking with other teenagers.

He really felt like a big shot now. And the other kids thought he was a big shot as well.

The next step was to impress the girls. There were many girls in his school that he liked and he wanted very much to impress them. One day he was invited to a party where there were many boys and girls. Some of the girls who were invited were just the ones that he wanted to impress. He brought his cigarettes and, as expected, when he started smoking a few of the girls started talking to him and thought that he was really "cool" because he smoked.

After a while Jeffrey started smoking so much that he couldn't stop. In fact, he got "hooked" on his cigarettes. He not only liked them, but found that he was very tense and nervous when he didn't have them. He began to smoke so much that he never went anywhere without his cigarettes. That was fine with him because he thought it really meant that he was now a grownup.

One day Jeffrey saw a girl in the hall at school whom he *really* liked. She was very pretty. When he overheard her talking to her friends, he liked the sound of her voice. In fact, it sounded like music to him. When he went home that day, Jeffrey began thinking about ways to meet this girl.

The next day, he found out from a friend that her name was Julie. Jeffrey couldn't get her out of his mind. Every day he thought more and more about Julie. He realized that he had fallen in love with her and it bothered him very much that he didn't know her better.

Finally, one day he got up the courage to sit next to her in the lunchroom. As they spoke Jeffrey realized that she was not only a very good student, but a very smart girl as well. Jeffrey wanted to ask her to take a

walk with him after school, but he was scared that she would say no. So he didn't ask her.

After that he did everything possible to meet Julie. He tried very hard to be where she was. He learned where she would be each day and made it his business to be there. And in this way he got to know her better.

Finally, one morning he got up the courage to ask her to take a walk with him after school. Julie agreed to meet him at 3 o'clock in front of the main gate of the school. Jeffrey's heart pounded with joy when she said yes. All day he could think of nothing else but meeting with Julie that afternoon. He knew that Julie was not as excited about him as he was about her, and he kept thinking about what he could do to make her like him more. Finally, 3 o'clock came. He raced to the school entrance and there was Julie.

As they walked away from school, Jeffrey got very nervous. He kept thinking of ways to impress Julie. He figured that one way of impressing her would be to start smoking a cigarette. That, he was sure, would really turn her on. That, he was positive, would really cause her to be interested in him. So he took out a cigarette. When he put it to his lips, he glanced sideways at Julie to see how impressed she would be. He was a little disappointed when she did not seem to be admiring him.

He then lit up the cigarette. As soon as he took his first puff Julie said, "Could you please put out that cigarette. I'm not a smoker and it makes me very uncomfortable."

Poor Jeffrey was shattered. He could hardly believe what was happening. "There must be something wrong with this girl," he said to himself, "She doesn't seem to be impressed with my smoking." And so he said, "What are you, too chicken to smoke?"

Julie replied, "I don't think it's chicken not to smoke. In fact, I think it's a pretty dumb habit. First of all, it's very unhealthy."

"I don't believe all that stuff about smoking causing cancer and other diseases," replied Jeffrey. "I know lots of people who are very old, have smoked for years, and haven't gotten sick."

"That still doesn't prove it's healthy," said Julie. "All that proves to me is that there are some people who were lucky enough to get away without being harmed. Just because a few don't get sick from cigarettes doesn't mean that no one gets sick from smoking."

Jeffrey didn't want to admit it, but inside he knew that what Julie said was true. "Well, I'm sure that I won't be one of those who gets sick," answered Jeffery.

"I hope for your sake you're right," said Julie, "but one can never be certain about things like this. I think that you think that everyone is admiring you when you smoke. Isn't that right?'' said Julie.

"Yes," said Jeffrey, "I'm sure of that."

"Well, I've got news for you," said Julie. "There are lots of people who not only don't admire smokers, but think it's a dumb habit and they're turned off by people who smoke. They don't think you're big and smart for smoking, but simple-minded."

Jeffrey was struck, as if by thunder. "I don't believe what you've said. Why *all* the kids look up to me when I smoke."

"You're wrong," said Julie. "Not all people, just some. Others are turned off and don't tell you. They just think that you're foolish and walk away. After all, any fool can smoke a cigarette. It's no great feat. It's not the kind of thing that should get real respect. Only *real* accomplishments deserve real respect. If you were a good student, or good at sports, or played an instrument well, or did something else that really required skill and effort, I'd have much more respect for you."

Jeffrey was shattered. He had never heard anything like that before. He didn't want to believe Julie, but he knew that she was a smart girl and that she was someone who should be taken seriously. Jeffrey was so upset by what Julie had said, and so disappointed that she didn't admire him for his smoking, that he felt like he was going to cry. So he excused himself and said that he had forgotten that he had to go home early that day, and he then left. As he walked home he felt very sad and lonely.

That night Jeffrey kept thinking about what Julie had said. He just couldn't get her words out of his mind. He just couldn't believe that there were people who thought smokers weren't big shots, but rather that they were dumb and simple-minded. He thought about all the time he had spent in the bathroom learning how to smoke instead of studying and practicing his sports. It was true that his grades had fallen. But the friends he spent time with often laughed at those who had high marks and called them "sissies" and "fags" and other bad names.

The next day Jeffrey again saw Julie. He liked her very much and knew that if he took out his cigarettes she wouldn't like him. So he decided that he would try to do something else to impress her. But he didn't know exactly what. She had told him that she liked boys who did well in school, but he couldn't talk much about that because he hadn't paid much attention in school lately. She had also said that she liked boys who were good at sports, but he was out of practice since he had started smoking. In fact, smoking made him short of breath and so he wasn't good at sports anymore, even when he tried. Julie had said that she liked people who played musical instruments, but he had never wanted to go to the trouble of learning how to play one.

And so, as he was walking with Julie, he found he had practically nothing to talk about. Although he would have liked to have spoken about the things Julie was interested in, he didn't have much to say on any of the subjects she liked. He began to be scared that Julie was finding him boring. She was too polite to tell him, but that was exactly how she was feeling. When they said good-bye he had a sinking feeling in his heart. He feared that Julie wouldn't want to see him again. And that was also true.

The next day Jeffrey went to the lunchroom in order to be with Julie. He was very unhappy to see her having lunch with Bill. Bill was one of the best students in the class. He also had many other interests. He was a good soccer player and he liked to draw. In fact, some of his cartoons were printed in the school paper. Jeffrey could tell that Julie was very interested in what Bill was saying and that she was having a very good time with him. It

was obvious also that Bill liked Julie as well. As Jeffrey watched them talking, he knew that he had absolutely no chance of Julie's liking him as much as she liked Bill.

Jeffrey was very upset. He was so upset that he couldn't concentrate in school for the rest of the day. So he learned practically nothing. When he went home, Jeffrey got very angry. He looked at his cigarettes and got even angrier. Suddenly, he took his cigarettes and

screamed, "Damn butts. I hate you." And he then threw them into his wastebasket with all his might.

After that, Jeffrey thought more and more about what had happened to him. He realized what a fool he had been. He was amazed at how clearly he had remembered everything Julie had said about smoking and how right she was. He decided that he was going to quit. He knew that he was hooked on cigarettes and that it was going to be very hard. He knew that he would be very nervous and tense when he didn't smoke, but he also knew that he just had to quit. He knew that he had to break the habit. It was very hard and it took many weeks. Many times he could think of nothing else but smoking. But he didn't give in to the desire and he finally broke the habit.

After that, Jeffrey started studying again. It wasn't easy because he had lost a lot of time and had missed much work. But he was a smart boy and worked very hard. Finally he caught up to the other boys and girls in his class. He also got back to playing basketball, his favorite sport. Now that he wasn't smoking any more, he didn't get short of breath and he played much better. He also found that his old friends were no longer interested in him. They said he was turning into a "goody-goody" for studying so much and began laughing at him. At first, Jeffrey felt bad about this, but he gradually realized that there was something wrong with them for laughing at someone who is trying to learn and improve himself. Besides, he began to make new friends and so didn't miss his old friends at all. His new friends

were boys and girls who were much more like Julie and Bill. He found these boys and girls much more interesting and much more fun. And as for Julie, she became Bill's girlfriend.

Even after Jeffrey had changed—and it took a long time—Julie continued to be Bill's girlfriend. However, Jeffrey became friendly with Julie's girlfriend Sue and they spent wonderful times together.

Lessons:

1. You usually respect most those accomplishments obtained from hard work. That which is easily accomplished, quickly learned, or not particularly a feat does not warrant true respect.

2. Smokers may think that they look like big shots, but there are many who think that they are stupid for what they are doing.
3. Learn from your experiences.

JENNIFER THE "SCAREDY -CAT"

Jennifer was scared of doing many things. She was so scared of so many things that the other kids used to call her "scaredy-cat."

For example, when all the other boys and girls were swimming, she was not only afraid to dive into the water from high places, but even from *low* places. She was scared that she might drown. Everybody told her that the pool where they swam was very safe and that no one had ever drowned in it. But this didn't help her feel less frightened. So she didn't go into the water at all. While the other kids were having fun in the water,

she just sat on the shore and wished that she weren't so scared. Although she was sad and lonely as she sat there, she still didn't try to go into the water.

She was afraid of other things as well. She was afraid of crowds and noisy places. She was scared of wide, open places and small, closed places. She was scared of heights and she was scared of deep tunnels. She was especially afraid of thunder and lightning, which just terrified her. And she was afraid to speak up in front of others, especially if the group was large. She was sure she would say something stupid and that everyone would laugh at her. Jennifer was particularly afraid of anything that was new or different. She never knew what was going to happen in new situations and that was very frightening to her. Because of all these fears, Jennifer hardly did anything with others and spent most of her time alone.

One day Jennifer was invited to another girl's birthday party. The invitation said: "Please come to my birthday party. We will play games, sing songs, and have good things to eat like ice cream and cake. Please tell me whether or not you plan to come."

Jennifer *really* wanted to go to that party. In fact, there was nothing in the whole world she wanted to do more than go to that party. A lot of the other children she knew would be there. She had already heard many boys and girls talking about it and had hoped that she would get an invitation. Now that the invitation had come, she didn't know what to do. As she sat in front of her house, reading the invitation, she got so upset that she began to cry. A teen-ager named Tom who was passing by could not help overhearing her. "What are you crying about?" asked Tom. "You sure look upset."

"I got this invitation to go to this great party and I'm afraid to go," cried Jennifer. "I want to go very much, but I'm very, very scared."

"Just what is it you're afraid of?" asked Tom.

"Everything," cried Jennifer. "I've never been to a party before."

"Everybody's scared of new things," said Tom.

"I didn't know that," said Jennifer. "Are you really telling me the truth?"

"Yes, it's really true," said the teen-ager. "You're no different from anyone else when it comes to being scared of new things. The main difference between you and others is that others *do* things that they're afraid of so they get used to them. Then they aren't scared any more."

"That's the hard part," said Jennifer.

"I know it," answered Tom. "But if you don't push yourself to do the things you're scared of, you'll always be scared and you'll have very little fun. You'll be very lonely and you'll lead a safe but dull and boring life."

Jennifer knew that what Tom had said was true. "Isn't there anything you can do to help me be less scared when I push myself?" asked Jennifer.

"You've just got to get up the courage to do the things you're scared to do," said the teen-ager. "I can tell you some important things, however, that may be of help to you. One is that scary things usually aren't as frightening as you think they will be. But you can't know that until you've done the scary thing. Also, every time you do something you're afraid of, it's a little less frightening."

Then as he started to leave Tom said, "Think about the things I've said to you. If you do, I think you'll agree that they make sense. And if you try to do the things I've suggested, I think you'll find that I'm right." Tom then waved good-bye to Jennifer and went on his way.

Finally, after thinking about what Tom had said a long, long time, Jennifer decided to try to push herself and not let her fears get the best of her. She decided that she *would* go to the party.

As the day of the party got closer, she got more and more scared. But she kept repeating to herself what Tom had said: "Scary things usually aren't as frightening as you think they will be, but you can't know that until you've done the scary thing. And every time you do the thing you're afraid of, it becomes a little less frightening." Over and over again she kept saying to herself: "Every time you do the thing you're afraid of, it becomes less and less frightening."

On the night before the party, Jennifer was so frightened that she could hardly fall asleep. She just lay in bed thinking about the party the next day. Sometimes she would think of the fun she might have and this made her feel very good. Then she would think of how scared she might be at the party and she would feel very sad and frightened. Finally, she fell asleep.

When she got up the next day, the first thing Jennifer thought of was that this was the day of the party. The very thought made her scared, but she was determined to go—no matter how scared she felt.

As she walked toward the party her teeth began to chatter and her knees started to knock together. She still forced herself to walk on toward the house where the party was. She kept saying to herself that the only way to stop being afraid of something was to do the frightening thing and that every time she did the scary thing it would become less and less scary.

When Jennifer got to the party, she was shaking so that she could hardly keep her finger still on the door bell. And when she walked into the house her legs were

shaking so that she tripped over her own feet and almost fell on her face. She was so scared then that she thought she'd wet her pants—but she didn't.

Once at the party, Jennifer began to see that the things that Tom, the teen-ager, had told her were true. First, she realized that scary things weren't as frightening as she thought they would be. Here she was at the party and it wasn't as frightening as she had thought it would be. In fact, most of the things the children were doing were fun!

And the more things she did, the more she thought about the fun she was having and the less she thought about her fears. Once again, Tom was right: The more you do a scary thing, the less frightening it becomes. Before she knew what had happened, the party was over. She had had such a good time that she hardly noticed how fast the time had passed.

The next time Jennifer went to a party, she was less scared. And each time she went, she became less and less scared. Finally the time came when she wasn't afraid of parties at all. This is what happened with her other fears as well. After getting up the courage to push herself to do the thing that frightened her, she found that it wasn't as scary as she had thought. And each time she did the scary thing it was less frightening.

One by one Jennifer did the things that she was afraid to do, and one by one she became less scared of doing these things. Finally, the day came when Jennifer had no more fears than anyone else, and she tried everything like all the other boys and girls. Then no one called her "scaredy-cat" any more.

Lessons:
1) All new things are scary and everyone is scared of them—at least a little bit.
2) Courage is pushing yourself to do a frightening thing that you know is important to do.
3) Scary things are usually not as frightening as you think they will be, but you can't know this until you try to do them.
4) Every time you do something that you're afraid of, it becomes a little less frightening. And if you do it enough times, it may no longer scare you at all.
5) Those who never push themselves to do scary things lead safe but dull, boring, and lonely lives.

CAMP
SIGHTS

It was Beth's first summer at camp. She was having a wonderful time. She learned to swim.

She made beautiful things in arts and crafts.

And at night she and the other campers sang around the campfire.

Best of all, she made a new friend. Her name was
Kathy and the two girls liked each·other very much.

They always tried to be on the same side when teams were chosen. They were swimming buddies. And they had lots of fun sharing secrets in their secret hiding place in the woods.

One day another girl in their bunk, Nancy, got sick and had to go to the camp infirmary. There, Doctor Robinson and Miss Clark, his nurse, took care of Nancy and the other sick campers.

Kathy decided to visit Nancy. As she got close to the infirmary she noticed that one of the windows was open. She thought it might be fun to peek inside. She

didn't know that she was peeking into the examination room. When she looked in she saw the doctor examining a boy. He wasn't wearing anything! She could even see his penis!

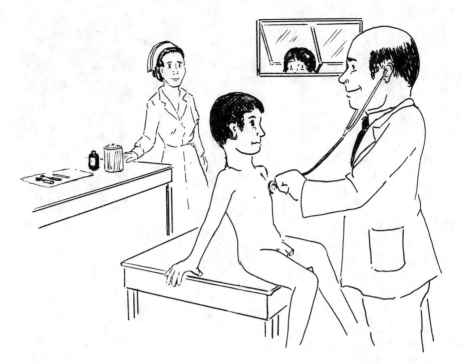

Kathy couldn't take her eyes off the boy's penis. But she was scared at the same time. She wanted to keep watching but she was afraid someone would see her. She looked for another minute and then thought, "Wait 'till I tell Beth about this!" She then ran as fast as she could to look for Beth.

When she found Beth she could hardly catch her breath, she had been running so fast. "Beth," she said, "you must come with me quickly to our secret hiding place. I've got the greatest secret in the whole world to tell you but I can't tell you here."

"What is it?" asked Beth. "What's the secret?"

"I can't tell you until we get to our secret hiding place," answered Kathy. "It's such a big secret that I can't tell you anywhere else."

Beth couldn't stand not knowing. "Please tell me," she begged. But Kathy insisted that she wait.

"No," said Kathy, "it's too dangerous. Someone might hear us. We're wasting time." And the two girls ran to the hiding place as fast as they could.

When they finally got to the secret hiding place, Kathy whispered so that no one could hear, "Do you promise you'll never tell anyone in the whole world?"

"Cross my heart and hope to die," answered Beth.

"Do you promise you'll keep it a secret for your whole life?" asked Kathy.

"I swear a thousand million times," answered Beth. "Please tell me."

"Well," said Kathy, as she whispered very low into Beth's ear, "do you know the infirmary where Nancy is?"

"Yes," said Beth, "what about it?"

"Well, they've got a little room there where they examine kids," whispered Kathy even lower.

"Yeah, yeah," said Beth, "I know about it."

"The window there was open and I saw Doctor Robinson examining a boy there," said Kathy, "and he wasn't wearing *anything*."

"Nothing at all?" said Beth.

"Nothing at all," answered Kathy, and then she whispered very low, so that Beth could hardly hear her, "I even saw his. . ."

"His what?" asked Beth. Kathy had spoken so low that Beth couldn't even hear her.

"His penis," said Kathy, and she began to giggle.

This time, Beth heard her and she too began to giggle.

"What did it look like?" asked Beth.

"It was just like my brother's but it was a little bigger," said Kathy.

"I don't have any brothers," said Beth, "and my father never lets me see his. He always closes the door when he undresses or when he goes to the bathroom. You have all the luck."

"If you promise to be my best friend for ever and ever," said Kathy, "I'll take you with me tomorrow to look in the window again."

"Oh, I promise, I promise," said Beth. "I'll be your best friend in the whole world forever and ever."

"Okay," said Kathy, "tomorrow morning, after breakfast, we'll tell everyone that we're going down to the infirmary to visit Nancy and then we'll peek in the window. I think the doctor examines all the sick children right after breakfast."

"You're the best friend in the whole world," said Beth. And the two girls ran back to camp.

That night they could hardly sleep, thinking about the next day. They giggled and whispered so much that the other children got annoyed at them. But they wouldn't tell their secret.

The next morning, after breakfast, they slowly walked toward the infirmary. They felt like running but they knew it was important to act like nothing special was going on. They didn't want to attract attention.

When they got to the infirmary, they saw that the window was still open—just the way it had been the day before. They tiptoed up to the window. They were care-

ful not to say a word. They hardly breathed. They were
also very scared.

When they looked inside they saw Doctor Robinson
examining a little girl.

"Just my luck," whispered Beth in a very low voice. "It's only a girl."

"Let's wait," said Kathy, "Maybe he'll examine a boy next."

Although it took the doctor only a few minutes to finish examining the little girl, it seemed like hours to Beth and Kathy. Finally, the next patient came in and it was the very same boy Kathy had seen the day before. As the boy started to undress they thought they would burst with excitement. Just as he was about to take off his pants, Kathy heard footsteps coming toward them. Quick as a wink she turned around and there she saw her counselor Marie coming toward them!

Kathy whispered into Beth's ear, "It's Marie! Let's get out of here." And fast as lightening the two girls ran back to their bunk.

When they got back to their bunk, they both hoped that Marie wouldn't have figured out what they had been doing. They were scared. They knew that she would soon be there. They knew that there was no way to hide from her or run away from her.

"So, young ladies," said Marie, when she came into the bunk, "what was going on down at the infirmary? What was so interesting to see inside that window?"

"Oh, nothing," said Kathy, "we were just passing by."

"Yes," said Beth, "we were just passing by."

"Don't lie to me," said Marie. "You were watching the doctor examine patients."

The two girls knew that there was no way to get out of it. Marie had seen them and knew what they had been doing. They felt awful. They felt ashamed. There was a long silence. It seemed like hours, although it was less than a minute. Finally, Marie said, "I'm not going to punish you. Instead, I'm going to take you both

down to speak to Doctor Robinson and Miss Clark. They know better than I what to do with children who do such terrible things."

When Beth and Kathy heard that, both girls began to cry. "I don't want to go," sobbed Kathy.

"Please don't make us go," cried Beth.

"I'm sorry girls," said Marie sternly. "We just can't allow things like this to go on. Now come with me. The sooner we get this over with, the better." And off they went to the infirmary.

When they came into the infirmary, Doctor Robinson said, "So what have we here?"

"Tell them what you've done, girls," said Marie. Kathy and Beth burst into tears. They were crying so hard they couldn't even talk.

"Go ahead, tell them" said Marie again.

"Why don't you tell us what happened?" said Doctor Robinson to Marie.

"I caught the two of them peeking through the window while you were examining patients," said Marie.

"Is that all?" said Miss Clark. She was very surprised.

"And that's what all this fuss is about?" said Doctor Robinson.

"Yes," said Marie, "I think what they've done is terrible."

"Well," said Doctor Robinson, "I don't agree with you. Most girls are interested in seeing what boys look like when they're undressed and boys are interested in seeing what girls look like. This is normal curiosity. There's nothing wrong with it. It's normal to *want* to see naked boys once in a while—and even to find it fun. However," Doctor Robinson said as he turned to the girls, "you just can't look at nude people as much as you'd like. When you get older you'll have more chances to see naked people. You'll have a boyfriend or get married, and then you'll be able to see naked boys and men more than you can now."

"I agree with Doctor Robinson," said Miss Clark to the girls. "I see nothing wrong in your *wanting* to see what boys look like when they're undressed. Peeking in windows, however, is another thing. Perhaps someday people will show their bodies more. But until that time you'll have to be content to live with the rules that tell when and where you can see other people naked. These are respectful of both people's desire to see and people's right to privacy. You just can't see every naked person you want to, but as you grow older you'll have more chances to."

"You mean we didn't do such a terrible thing," said Kathy.

"No," answered Doctor Robinson, "you didn't do anything terrible."

Beth wanted to be sure that she understood. "You mean it's normal to *want* to see people undressed? But you can't go around trying to see them undressed whenever you want. Is that right?" she asked.

"Yes, that's right," said Miss Clark. "You can't go around peeking at anyone you want to. When you're older or when you're married you'll have plenty of chances to see naked boys and men. But even then, you won't be able to whenever you want. Just sometimes."

Kathy and Beth began to smile. They felt relieved. They didn't feel so terrible about themselves any more.

Marie then spoke to the doctor and nurse. "I know you're really right. Once in a while, when I was younger,

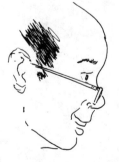 

I used to try to see boys naked; but I thought it was a bad thing, and I didn't want Kathy and Beth to be doing the same kinds of bad things. I know it's normal to want to do it, but children just can't. They have to wait until they're older."

"So we're not going to get punished?" Beth asked Marie.

"Not this time," answered Marie. "But that doesn't mean you won't be punished if you go peeking into the infirmary window again. That's still against the rules of the camp."

"That's right," said Miss Clark. "You can't peek into the infirmary window."

"...Even though it's perfectly normal and healthy to want to do it once in a while," said Doctor Robinson as he led Marie and the two girls out the infirmary door.

"Let's be a little more careful about closing that examining room window," said Doctor Robinson to Miss Clark. "We don't want to be attracting any crowds," he said as he left the infirmary.

Lessons:
1) Most girls like to see naked boys, and most boys like to see naked girls. Most women like to see naked men, and most men like to see naked women. This is normal and, in my opinion, there's nothing wrong with wanting to see others naked.
2) You can't see other people naked as much as or as often as you might like. But the older you get, the more chances you'll have.
3) Show respect for other people's right to privacy and they are more likely to show respect for yours.

LEO
THE
LIAR

Leo was a liar. Often, if Leo had a choice between telling the truth and telling a lie, he would lie. One of the reasons for this was that his parents often lied and so he had learned the habit from them. They were the kind of people that tried to cover up their faults by lying about them. They were the kind of people who tried to make everyone think that they were better than others by making up stories—stories about things they never did. They rarely admitted their faults. They told all kinds of tales about exciting adventures they never even had. And that's where Leo learned to lie.

One day, someone told Leo that lying was bad, that it was wrong, and that God would punish him for lying. At first, this scared Leo very much. He kept walking around worrying about God punishing him. He also

kept worrying about what kind of punishment God might give him. He waited and waited and worried and worried, but no punishment came from God. He continued to lie and nothing particularly bad happened to him. He knew a few other children who lied a lot, and it didn't appear to him that God was punishing them either! So he finally decided that either there was no God, or if there was one, he wasn't punishing liars—at least God wasn't punishing Leo.

One day Leo's parents told him that they were going to get a divorce. He didn't believe the reasons they gave

him, because they were both such liars that he didn't trust most of the things they said. This made things very difficult for Leo because he really wanted to know what had happened. He really wanted to understand why they were getting divorced. He asked them more questions, but he still didn't get what he felt were honest answers. So he just gave up on asking questions, got disgusted with them, and decided he couldn't believe a word of what they were saying—even when they told the truth.

Leo figured that his parents must have been ashamed about something with regard to the divorce. And so he decided not to tell anyone about it. When others talked about their parents, Leo talked about his as if they were still married and living together at home. However, Leo stopped inviting the other kids to his house because he feared that they would find out about his big secret. And when children asked to visit him, he would make up some kind of an excuse for not inviting them over. Leo started spending less and less time with his friends, because he was scared that they would find out that his parents had gotten divorced.

Now there really wasn't anything for Leo to be ashamed about when his parents had gotten divorced. But because they were covering it up, he thought that there *was* something to be ashamed about. And his lying about it caused him a new problem, in addition to the problem of his parents' divorce. The new problem was that he was always scared that his friends would discover his lie. Unfortunately, walking around scared that someone would find out the truth still did not stop him from lying.

Another thing that Leo used to lie about was his grades. He was always telling other children about the high marks he got in school. Actually, he got very low marks because he didn't pay attention to the teacher and never did very much homework. Because he was careful never to show anyone his test papers, the other children began to suspect that he was lying about his high marks. Also, he hardly ever gave right answers when the teacher called on him in class. This too made everyone think that he was a liar.

One day Leo dropped one of his books in the school hallway. The book had a lot of his old tests in it. Most of the marks were Ds and Fs. Unfortunately for Leo, a girl in his class found the book, opened it up, and saw all the poor grades. It wasn't long before everyone else

in the class knew about the kind of marks Leo was getting. And it wasn't long before everyone started laughing at him and calling him "liar." This made him feel very bad and ashamed. What was worse, no one believed him after that even when he told the truth. Just as he had stopped believing his parents because they had lied—even when they told the truth—Leo's friends stopped believing him, even when he told the truth.

Another problem that Leo had with his lying was trying to remember all the different lies. It was hard to keep them all straight! He spent a lot of time trying to

remember to whom he had told which particular lie. He was often afraid that he would make a mistake and tell the wrong lie to the wrong person! And this is exactly what happened. Then the other children started laughing at him and saying, "Leo, you're getting your lies all mixed up." Leo decided that his memory just wasn't good enough for him to be a good liar. Actually, what he didn't realize was that no one's memory is good enough to be a good liar. Those who tell the truth don't have to keep extra things on their minds—things about which lies they told to whom. And they don't have to worry about getting all their lies straight.

One morning Leo stole thirty dollars from his teacher's purse. Ms. Lane was one of the best teachers in the whole school and all the children loved her very much. By mistake, she had left her purse in the back of the room, right near Leo's seat. While everyone was listening to her, Leo stole some money from her purse.

That afternoon Ms. Lane was very upset. She told the class that some money was missing from her purse and she was quite sure that someone in the class had done it. She was so upset that she began to cry, right in front of the class. Everyone in the class was also very upset. Ms. Lane had been very nice to Leo, and Leo started to feel very bad about what he had done. He had begun to feel sorry that he had stolen the money. Ms. Lane said that over the next few days she was going to speak to every child, in private, to try to find out who stole the money.

When Leo's turn came, he was a little scared. He also still felt bad about himself for what he had done. But he was such a good liar, and had done it for so long, that he was able to convince Ms. Lane that he hadn't stolen her money, even though he had. Although Leo got away with having stolen the money, and al-

though he had managed to get his teacher to believe that he hadn't stolen it, he still felt bad about himself.

He felt bad that he had stolen the money, and he felt bad that he had lied. For the next few days Leo was in a very bad mood. He was unhappy and cranky and, worst of all, he just felt bad about himself for what he had done.

After that Leo was very sad and lonely. Ms. Lane was such a nice person and everybody spoke about how terrible it was that someone had stolen money from Ms. Lane—one of the best and nicest teachers in the school. Every time he heard children saying these things, he felt even worse about himself.

Finally, one day Leo could stand it no longer. He stayed after school and confessed to Ms. Lane that he had stolen her money. Ms. Lane told Leo that she

wasn't surprised that it was he who had stolen her money because he had such a reputation for being a liar. But now, he had stolen as well as lied. Now he had added a new problem to the old one.

"Well," said Ms. Lane, "what do you think we can do about these problems?"

Leo answered, "I'd like to try to give you back the money that I stole. Of the thirty dollars that I took, I still have eight dollars left and I could work to earn the rest. If you'll let me do that, I know I won't feel so terrible about what I've done to you."

"And you'll feel better about yourself as well," said Ms. Lane.

"I know that," said Leo. "I go around feeling guilty all the time, feeling bad about myself for what I did."

"You seem to have been punished already for the theft," said the teacher. "Maybe you don't need another punishment."

"Are you saying that you're not going to punish me?" asked Leo.

"Well," said Ms. Lane, "if you keep your promise and return all my money, and if you have truly learned an important lesson from this experience, I don't see how there's anything further to be gained by punishing you. If, however, you didn't feel guilty—if you didn't suffer with bad feelings about yourself for what you've done—I would punish you to help you remember not to steal again. Because you've already been punished by the bad feelings you have about yourself, I don't think that anything will be accomplished by punishing you further. I think you've learned a lesson about stealing—a lesson that may help you stop doing it."

"I'm sure I have," said Leo. "And I'm going to get that money back to you as fast as I can."

"I hope I can believe you," said Ms. Lane.

"Are you saying you don't believe me?" said Leo.

"You certainly sound sincere now," said Ms. Lane, "but you sounded sincere when you told me that you hadn't stolen my money. You've learned to be a very convincing liar."

"But you've *got* to believe me," said Leo. "I *really* mean what I'm saying."

"I'd be a fool if I believed you entirely," said the teacher. "Because of all your lying, practically no one believes most of the things you say. When I get the money back, then I'll start to believe you."

Leo felt bad about what Ms. Lane had said, but he knew that what she said was true. "Then how can I get people to believe me?" he asked.

"Only by changing your reputation. Only by proving by what you *do,* rather than what you *say,* can you change your reputation. It's only by telling the truth many times that you will be trusted."

"But that can take a long time," said Leo.

"Of course," said Ms. Lane. "Trusting someone doesn't take place suddenly. It has to grow over time. It only comes with many experiences which prove that the person can be trusted."

"I don't like to think of it that way. I want you to trust me *now*," said Leo.

"I understand, but I suggest we talk about this more *after* you've brought back my money." said Ms. Lane. "As they say, 'Talk is cheap,' That is, it's much easier to *talk* about doing something than actually doing it. Doing something is much harder than talking about it. I'll trust you when you've proven that you *can* be trusted." With this comment, Ms. Lane said goodbye to Leo.

The next day Leo came to Ms. Lane after school and returned the eight dollars of her money that he hadn't yet spent. She said, "Now I'm starting to trust you a little bit, because you're starting to prove to me that your promises will be kept. But you've got a long way to go."

"Believe me," said Leo, "I'll keep the rest of my promises and return the twenty-two dollars I still owe you. I feel better when I tell the truth than when I lie. Also, I don't have to keep worrying about other people finding out about my lies."

"I'm glad to hear you say that," said Ms. Lane. "It seems to me that you're learning some very useful things. I think we should talk more about them *after* you've returned the rest of my money. As I said to you before, talk is cheap."

So, Leo worked very hard during the next few weeks. He mowed lawns and babysat. The lawn mowing, espe-

cially, was very hard work, but he finally earned the twenty-two dollars and gave it to Ms. Lane.

When Leo gave Ms. Lane the money, she thanked him and said, "Well, Leo, you certainly are changing your reputation with me. You're proving to me that you *can* keep your promises. I'm sure you'll be pleased to learn, too, that other children in the class have told me that you're changing. They're coming to believe you more and more."

"I'm glad," said Leo. "I've come to realize how much I used to worry about which lies I told to which people. It was very hard to keep them all straight. I just don't have that good a memory."

"No one does," said Ms. Lane.

"I didn't realize that," said Leo.

"Well,' said Ms. Lane, "it appears to me that you've learned some very useful things in the last few weeks— things that I hope will continue to help you stop lying."

"I think they will," said Leo. "But as you say, 'Talk is cheap.' I'm going to have to prove it to you again before you'll really trust me."

"That's right," said Ms. Lane. "Let's see if you can. By the end of the school year, I think we'll know whether or not you can keep up this new life style."

Over the next few months, Leo worked hard at telling the truth. He began to realize that his parents had set a bad example for him and were the ones who had taught him to lie in the first place. With Ms. Lane's help, he had come to see how foolish the lying was and how many new problems he had caused for himself by not telling the truth.

By the end of the year, Leo had many friends, had changed his reputation, and was no longer sad and lonely. People liked Leo, and most important of all, Leo liked himself.

Lessons:
1) Liars often have to go around worrying a lot that others will discover the truth.
2) When everyone finds out that a person is a liar, the liar isn't believed—even when he or she tells the truth.
3) Liars need very good memories to keep all their lies straight—and no one's memory is so good that he or she can keep many lies straight.
4) No one likes a liar—and liars usually don't even like themselves.
5) Real trust cannot be gained quickly. It only comes slowly with much proof that the person can be trusted.